Walking

Walking

BY

Henry David Thoreau

KALPAZ

ISBN: 978-93-5128-509-0

First Published in 1862
Indian Reprint in 2017

Published by

Kalpaz Publications
C-30, Satyawati Nagar,
Delhi – 110052
E-mail: kalpaz@hotmail.com
Website: kalpazpublications.com
Ph.: +91-9212142040

Cataloging in Publication Data—DK
Courtesy: D.K. Agencies (P) Ltd. <docinfo@dkagencies.com>

Thoreau, Henry David, 1817-1862, **author.**
Walking / Henry David Thoreau.
pages cm
"First published in 1982"—Title page verso.
ISBN 9789351285090

1. Walking. 2. Nature. I. Title.

PS3051.W35 2017 DDC 814.3 23

Walking

I wish to speak a word for Nature, for absolute freedom and wildness, as contrasted with a freedom and culture merely civil—to regard man as an inhabitant, or a part and parcel of Nature, rather than a member of society. I wish to make an extreme statement, if so I may make an emphatic one, for there are enough champions of civilization: the minister and the school committee and every one of you will take care of that.

I have met with but one or two persons in the course of my life who understood the art of Walking, that is, of taking walks—who had a genius, so to speak, for SAUNTERING, which word is beautifully derived "from idle people who roved about the country, in the Middle Ages, and asked charity, under pretense of going a la Sainte Terre," to the Holy Land, till the children exclaimed, "There goes a Sainte-Terrer," a Saunterer, a Holy-Lander. They who never go to the Holy Land in their walks, as they pretend, are indeed mere idlers and vagabonds; but they who do go there are saunterers in the good sense, such as I mean. Some, however, would derive the word from sans terre without land or a home, which, therefore, in the good sense, will mean, having no particular home, but equally at home everywhere. For this is the secret of successful sauntering. He who sits still in a house all the time may be the greatest vagrant of all; but the saunterer, in the good sense, is no more vagrant than the meandering river, which is all the while sedulously seeking the shortest course to the sea. But I prefer the first, which, indeed, is the most probable derivation. For every walk is a sort of crusade, preached by some Peter the Hermit in us, to go forth and reconquer this Holy Land from the hands of the Infidels.

It is true, we are but faint-hearted crusaders, even the walkers, nowadays, who undertake no persevering, never-ending enterprises. Our expeditions are but tours, and come round again at evening to the old hearth-side from which we set out. Half the walk is but retracing our steps. We should go forth on the shortest walk, perchance, in the spirit of undying adventure, never to return— prepared to send back our embalmed hearts only as relics to our desolate kingdoms. If you are ready to leave father and mother, and brother and sister, and wife and child and friends, and never see them again—if you have paid your debts, and made your will, and settled all your affairs, and are a free man—then you are ready for a walk.

To come down to my own experience, my companion and I, for I sometimes have a companion, take pleasure in fancying ourselves knights of a new, or rather an old, order—not Equestrians or Chevaliers, not Ritters or Riders, but Walkers, a still more ancient and honorable class, I trust. The Chivalric and heroic spirit which once belonged to the Rider seems now to reside in, or perchance to have subsided into, the Walker—not the Knight, but Walker, Errant. He is a sort of fourth estate, outside of Church and State and People.

We have felt that we almost alone hereabouts practiced this noble art; though, to tell the truth, at least if their own assertions are to be received, most of my townsmen would fain walk sometimes, as I do, but they cannot. No wealth can buy the requisite leisure, freedom, and independence which are the capital in this profession. It comes only by the grace of God. It requires a direct dispensation from Heaven to become a walker. You must be born into the family of the Walkers. Ambulator nascitur, non fit. Some of my townsmen, it is true, can remember and have described to me some walks which they took ten years ago, in which they were so blessed as to lose themselves for half an hour in the woods; but I know very well that they have confined themselves to the highway ever since, whatever pretensions they may make to belong to this select class. No doubt they were elevated for a moment as by the reminiscence of a previous state of existence, when even they were foresters and outlaws.

"When he came to grene wode,
In a mery mornynge,
There he herde the notes small
Of byrdes mery syngynge.

"It is ferre gone, sayd Robyn,
That I was last here;
Me Lyste a lytell for to shote
At the donne dere."

I think that I cannot preserve my health and spirits, unless I spend four hours a day at least—and it is commonly more than that—sauntering through the woods and over the hills and fields, absolutely free from all worldly engagements. You may safely say, A penny for your thoughts, or a thousand pounds. When sometimes I am reminded that the mechanics and shopkeepers stay in their shops not only all the forenoon, but all the afternoon too, sitting with crossed legs, so many of them—as if the legs were made to sit upon, and not to stand or walk upon—I think that they deserve some credit for not having all committed suicide long ago.

I, who cannot stay in my chamber for a single day without acquiring some rust, and when sometimes I have stolen forth for a walk at the eleventh hour, or four o'clock in the afternoon, too late to redeem the day, when the shades of night were already beginning to be mingled with the daylight, have felt as if I had committed some sin to be atoned for,—I confess that I am astonished at the power of endurance, to say nothing of the moral insensibility, of my neighbors who confine themselves to shops and offices the whole day for weeks and months, aye, and years almost together. I know not what manner of stuff they are of—sitting there now at three o'clock in the afternoon, as if it were three o'clock in the morning. Bonaparte may talk of the three-o'clock-in-the-morning courage, but it is nothing to the courage which can sit down cheerfully at this hour in the afternoon over against one's self whom you have known all the morning, to starve out a garrison to whom you are bound by such strong ties of sympathy. I wonder that about this time, or say between four and five o'clock in the afternoon, too late for the morning papers and too early for the evening ones, there is not a general explosion heard up and down the street, scattering a legion of antiquated and house-bred notions and whims to the four winds for an airing-and so the evil cure itself.

How womankind, who are confined to the house still more than men, stand it I do not know; but I have ground to suspect that most of them do not STAND it at all. When, early in a summer afternoon, we have been shaking the dust of the village from the skirts of our garments, making haste past those houses with purely Doric or Gothic fronts, which have such an air of repose about them, my companion whispers that probably about these times their occupants are all gone to bed. Then it is that I appreciate the beauty and the glory of architecture, which itself never turns in, but forever stands out and erect, keeping watch over the slumberers.

No doubt temperament, and, above all, age, have a good deal to do with it. As a man grows older, his ability to sit still and follow indoor occupations increases. He grows vespertinal in his habits as the evening of life approaches, till at last he comes forth only just before sundown, and gets all the walk that he requires in half an hour.

But the walking of which I speak has nothing in it akin to taking exercise, as it is called, as the sick take medicine at stated hours—as the Swinging of dumb-bells or chairs; but is itself the enterprise and adventure of the day. If you would get exercise, go in search of the springs of life. Think of a man's swinging dumbbells for his health, when those springs are bubbling up in far-off pastures unsought by him!

Moreover, you must walk like a camel, which is said to be the only beast which ruminates when walking. When a traveler asked Wordsworth's servant to show him her master's study, she answered, "Here is his library, but his study is out of doors."

Living much out of doors, in the sun and wind, will no doubt produce a certain roughness of character—will cause a thicker cuticle to grow over some of the finer qualities of our nature, as on the face and hands, or as severe manual labor robs the hands of some of their delicacy of touch. So staying in the house, on the other hand, may produce a softness and smoothness, not to say thinness of skin, accompanied by an increased sensibility to certain impressions. Perhaps we should be more susceptible to some influences important to our intellectual and moral growth, if the sun had shone and the wind blown on us a little less; and no doubt it is a nice matter to proportion rightly the thick and thin skin. But methinks that is a scurf that will fall off fast enough—that the natural remedy is to be found in the proportion which the night bears to the day, the winter to the summer, thought to experience. There will be so much the more air and sunshine in our thoughts. The callous palms of the laborer are conversant with finer tissues of self-respect and heroism, whose touch thrills the heart, than the languid fingers of idleness. That is mere sentimentality that lies abed by day and thinks itself white, far from the tan and callus of experience.

When we walk, we naturally go to the fields and woods: what would become of us, if we walked only in a garden or a mall? Even some sects of philosophers have felt the necessity of importing the woods to themselves, since they did not go to the woods. "They planted groves and walks of Platanes," where they took subdiales ambulationes in porticos open to the air. Of course it is of no use to direct our steps to the woods, if they do not carry us thither. I am alarmed when it happens that I have walked a mile into the woods bodily, without getting there in spirit. In my afternoon walk I would fain forget all my morning occupations and my obligations to Society. But it sometimes happens that I cannot easily shake off the village. The thought of some work will run in my head and I am not where my body is—I am out of my senses. In my walks I would fain return to my senses. What business have I in the woods, if I am thinking of something out of the woods? I suspect myself, and cannot help a shudder when I find myself so implicated even in what are called good works—for this may sometimes happen.

My vicinity affords many good walks; and though for so many years I have walked almost every day, and sometimes for several days together, I have not yet exhausted them. An absolutely new prospect is a great happiness, and I can still get this any afternoon. Two or three hours' walking will carry me to as strange a country as I expect ever to see. A single farmhouse which I had not seen before is sometimes as good as the dominions of the King of Dahomey. There is in fact a sort of harmony discoverable between the capabilities of the landscape within a circle of ten miles' radius, or the limits of an afternoon walk, and the threescore years and ten of human life. It will never become quite familiar to you.

Nowadays almost all man's improvements, so called, as the building of houses and the cutting down of the forest and of all large trees, simply deform the landscape, and make it more and more tame and cheap. A people who would begin by burning the fences and let the forest stand! I saw the fences half consumed, their ends lost in the middle of the prairie, and some worldly miser with a surveyor looking after his bounds, while heaven had taken place around him, and he did not see the angels going to and fro, but was looking for an old post-hole in the midst of paradise. I looked again, and saw him standing in the middle of a boggy Stygian fen, surrounded by devils, and he had found his bounds without a doubt, three little stones, where a stake had been driven, and looking nearer, I saw that the Prince of Darkness was his surveyor.

I can easily walk ten, fifteen, twenty, any number of miles, commencing at my own door, without going by any house, without crossing a road except where the fox and the mink do: first along by the river, and then the brook, and then the meadow and the woodside. There are square miles in my vicinity which have no inhabitant. From many a hill I can see civilization and the abodes of man afar. The farmers and their works are scarcely more obvious than woodchucks and their burrows. Man and his affairs, church and state and school, trade and commerce, and manufactures and agriculture even politics, the most alarming of them all—I am pleased to see how little space they occupy in the landscape.

Politics is but a narrow field, and that still narrower highway yonder leads to it. I sometimes direct the traveler thither. If you would go to the political world, follow the great road—follow that market-man, keep his dust in your eyes, and it will lead you straight to it; for it, too, has its place merely, and does not occupy all space. I pass from it as from a bean field into the forest, and it is forgotten. In one half-hour I can walk off to some portion of the earth's surface where a man does not stand from one year's end to another, and there, consequently, politics are not, for they are but as the cigar-smoke of a man.

The village is the place to which the roads tend, a sort of expansion of the highway, as a lake of a river. It is the body of which roads are the arms and legs—a trivial or quadrivial place, the thoroughfare and ordinary of travelers. The word is from the Latin villa which together with via, a way, or more anciently ved and vella, Varro derives from veho, to carry, because the villa is the place to and from which things are carried. They who got their living by teaming were said vellaturam facere. Hence, too, the Latin word vilis and our vile, also villain. This suggests what kind of degeneracy villagers are liable to. They are wayworn by the travel that goes by and over them, without traveling themselves.

Some do not walk at all; others walk in the highways; a few walk across lots. Roads are made for horses and men of business. I do not travel in them much, comparatively, because I am not in a hurry to get to any tavern or grocery or livery-stable or depot to which they lead. I am a good horse to travel, but not from choice a roadster. The landscape-painter uses the figures of men to mark a road. He would not make that use of my figure. I walk out into a nature such as the old prophets and poets, Menu, Moses, Homer, Chaucer, walked in. You may name it America, but it is not America; neither Americus Vespueius, nor Columbus, nor the rest were the discoverers of it. There is a truer amount of it in mythology than in any history of America, so called, that I have seen.

However, there are a few old roads that may be trodden with profit, as if they led somewhere now that they are nearly discontinued. There is the Old Marlborough Road, which does not go to Marlborough now, methinks, unless that is Marlborough where it carries me. I am the bolder to speak of it here, because I presume that there are one or two such roads in every town.

THE OLD MARLBOROUGH ROAD

Where they once dug for money,
But never found any;
Where sometimes Martial Miles
Singly files,
And Elijah Wood,
I fear for no good:
No other man,
Save Elisha Dugan—
O man of wild habits,
Partridges and rabbits
Who hast no cares
Only to set snares,
Who liv'st all alone,
Close to the bone
And where life is sweetest
Constantly eatest.
When the spring stirs my blood
With the instinct to travel,
I can get enough gravel
On the Old Marlborough Road.
Nobody repairs it,
For nobody wears it;
It is a living way,
As the Christians say.
Not many there be
Who enter therein,
Only the guests of the
Irishman Quin.
What is it, what is it
But a direction out there,
And the bare possibility
Of going somewhere?
Great guide-boards of stone,

But travelers none;
Cenotaphs of the towns
Named on their crowns.
It is worth going to see
Where you MIGHT be.
What king
Did the thing,
I am still wondering;
Set up how or when,
By what selectmen,
Gourgas or Lee,
Clark or Darby?
They're a great endeavor
To be something forever;
Blank tablets of stone,
Where a traveler might groan,
And in one sentence
Grave all that is known
Which another might read,
In his extreme need.
I know one or two
Lines that would do,
Literature that might stand
All over the land
Which a man could remember
Till next December,
And read again in the spring,
After the thawing.
If with fancy unfurled
You leave your abode,
You may go round the world
By the Old Marlborough Road.

At present, in this vicinity, the best part of the land is not private property; the landscape is not owned, and the walker enjoys comparative freedom. But possibly the day will come when it will be partitioned off into so-called pleasure-grounds, in which a few will take a narrow and exclusive pleasure only—when fences shall be multiplied, and man-traps and other engines invented to confine men to the PUBLIC road, and walking over the surface of God's earth shall be construed to mean trespassing on some gentleman's grounds. To enjoy a thing exclusively is commonly to exclude yourself from the true enjoyment of it. Let us improve our opportunities, then, before the evil days come.

What is it that makes it so hard sometimes to determine whither we will walk? I believe that there is a subtle magnetism in Nature, which, if we unconsciously yield to it, will direct us aright. It is not indifferent to us which way we walk. There is a right way; but we are very liable from heedlessness and stupidity to take the wrong one. We would fain take that walk, never yet taken by us through this actual world, which is perfectly symbolical of the path which we love to travel in the interior and ideal world; and sometimes, no doubt, we find it difficult to choose our direction, because it does not yet exist distinctly in our idea.

When I go out of the house for a walk, uncertain as yet whither I will bend my steps, and submit myself to my instinct to decide for me, I find, strange and whimsical as it may seem, that I finally and inevitably settle southwest, toward some particular wood or meadow or deserted pasture or hill in that direction. My needle is slow to settle,—varies a few degrees, and does not always point due southwest, it is true, and it has good authority for this variation, but it always settles between west and south-southwest. The future lies that way to me, and the earth seems more unexhausted and richer on that side. The outline which would bound my walks would be, not a circle, but a parabola, or rather like one of those cometary orbits which have been thought to be non-returning curves, in this case opening westward, in which my house occupies the place of the sun. I turn round and round irresolute sometimes for a quarter of an hour, until I decide, for a thousandth time, that I will walk into the southwest or west. Eastward I go only by force; but westward I go free. Thither no business leads me. It is hard for me to believe that I shall find fair landscapes or sufficient wildness and freedom behind the eastern horizon. I am not excited by the prospect of a walk thither; but I believe that the forest which I see in the western horizon stretches uninterruptedly toward the setting sun, and there are no towns nor cities in it of enough consequence to disturb me. Let me live where I will, on this side is the city, on that the wilderness, and ever I am leaving the city more and more, and withdrawing into the wilderness. I should not lay so much stress on this fact, if I did not believe that something like this is the prevailing tendency of my countrymen. I must walk toward Oregon, and not toward Europe. And that way the nation is moving, and I may say that mankind progress from east to west. Within a few years we have witnessed the phenomenon of a southeastward migration, in the settlement of Australia; but this affects us as a retrograde movement, and, judging from the moral and physical character of the first generation of Australians, has not yet proved a successful experiment. The eastern Tartars think that there is nothing west beyond Thibet. "The world ends there," say they; "beyond there is nothing but a shoreless sea." It is unmitigated East where they live.

We go eastward to realize history and study the works of art and literature, retracing the steps of the race; we go westward as into the future, with a spirit of enterprise and adventure. The Atlantic is a Lethean stream, in our passage over which we have had an opportunity to forget the Old World and its institutions. If we do not succeed this time, there is perhaps one more chance for the race left before it arrives on the banks of the Styx; and that is in the Lethe of the Pacific, which is three times as wide.

I know not how significant it is, or how far it is an evidence of singularity, that an individual should thus consent in his pettiest walk with the general movement of the race; but I know that something akin to the migratory instinct in birds and quadrupeds—which, in some instances, is known to have affected the squirrel tribe, impelling them to a general and mysterious movement, in which they were seen, say some, crossing the broadest rivers, each on its particular chip, with its tail raised for a sail, and bridging narrower streams with their dead—that something like the furor which affects the domestic cattle in the spring, and which is referred to a worm in their tails,—affects both nations and individuals, either perennially or from time to time. Not a flock of wild geese cackles over our town, but it to some extent unsettles the value of real estate here, and, if I were a broker, I should probably take that disturbance into account.

"Than longen folk to gon on pilgrimages,
And palmeres for to seken strange strondes."

Every sunset which I witness inspires me with the desire to go to a West as distant and as fair as that into which the sun goes down. He appears to migrate westward daily, and tempt us to follow him. He is the Great Western Pioneer whom the nations follow. We dream all night of those mountain-ridges in the horizon, though they may be of vapor only, which were last gilded by his rays. The island of Atlantis, and the islands and gardens of the Hesperides, a sort of terrestrial paradise, appear to have been the Great West of the ancients, enveloped in mystery and poetry. Who has not seen in imagination, when looking into the sunset sky, the gardens of the Hesperides, and the foundation of all those fables?

Columbus felt the westward tendency more strongly than any before. He obeyed it, and found a New World for Castile and Leon. The herd of men in those days scented fresh pastures from afar,

> "And now the sun had stretched out all the hills,
> And now was dropped into the western bay;
> At last HE rose, and twitched his mantle blue;
> Tomorrow to fresh woods and pastures new."

Where on the globe can there be found an area of equal extent with that occupied by the bulk of our States, so fertile and so rich and varied in its productions, and at the same time so habitable by the European, as this is? Michaux, who knew but part of them, says that "the species of large trees are much more numerous in North America than in Europe; in the United States there are more than one hundred and forty species that exceed thirty feet in height; in France there are but thirty that attain this size." Later botanists more than confirm his observations. Humboldt came to America to realize his youthful dreams of a tropical vegetation, and he beheld it in its greatest perfection in the primitive forests of the Amazon, the most gigantic wilderness on the earth, which he has so eloquently described. The geographer Guyot, himself a European, goes farther— farther than I am ready to follow him; yet not when he says: "As the plant is made for the animal, as the vegetable world is made for the animal world, America is made for the man of the Old World.... The man of the Old World sets out upon his way. Leaving the highlands of Asia, he descends from station to station towards Europe. Each of his steps is marked by a new civilization superior to the preceding, by a greater power of development. Arrived at the Atlantic, he pauses on the shore of this unknown ocean, the bounds of which he knows not, and turns upon his footprints for an instant." When he has exhausted the rich soil of Europe, and reinvigorated himself, "then recommences his adventurous career westward as in the earliest ages." So far Guyot.

From this western impulse coming in contact with the barrier of the Atlantic sprang the commerce and enterprise of modern times. The younger Michaux, in his Travels West of the Alleghanies in 1802, says that the common inquiry in the newly settled West was, "'From what part of the world have you come?' As if these vast and fertile regions would naturally be the place of meeting and common country of all the inhabitants of the globe."

To use an obsolete Latin word, I might say, Ex Oriente lux; ex Occidente FRUX. From the East light; from the West fruit.

Sir Francis Head, an English traveler and a Governor-General of Canada, tells us that "in both the northern and southern hemispheres of the New World, Nature has not only outlined her works on a larger scale, but has painted the whole picture with brighter and more costly colors than she used in delineating and in beautifying the Old World.... The heavens of America appear infinitely higher, the sky is bluer, the air is fresher, the cold is intenser, the moon looks larger, the stars are brighter the thunder is louder, the lightning is vivider, the wind is stronger, the rain is heavier, the mountains are higher, the rivers longer, the forests bigger, the plains broader." This statement will do at least to set against Buffon's account of this part of the world and its productions.

Linnaeus said long ago, "Nescio quae facies laeta, glabra plantis Americanis" (I know not what there is of joyous and smooth in the aspect of American plants); and I think that in this country there are no, or at most very few, Africanae bestiae, African beasts, as the Romans called them, and that in this respect also it is peculiarly fitted for the habitation of man. We are told that within three miles of the center of the East-Indian city of Singapore, some of the inhabitants are annually carried off by tigers; but the traveler can lie down in the woods at night almost anywhere in North America without fear of wild beasts.

These are encouraging testimonies. If the moon looks larger here than in Europe, probably the sun looks larger also. If the heavens of America appear infinitely higher, and the stars brighter, I trust that these facts are symbolical of the height to which the philosophy and poetry and religion of her inhabitants may one day soar. At length, perchance, the immaterial heaven will appear as much higher to the American mind, and the intimations that star it as much brighter. For I believe that climate does thus react on man—as there is something in the mountain air that feeds the spirit and inspires. Will not man grow to greater perfection intellectually as well as physically under these influences? Or is it unimportant how many foggy days there are in his life? I trust that we shall be more imaginative, that our thoughts will be clearer, fresher, and more ethereal, as our sky—our understanding more comprehensive and broader, like our plains—our intellect generally on a grander seale, like our thunder and lightning, our rivers and mountains and forests-and our hearts shall even correspond in breadth and depth and grandeur to our inland seas. Perchance there will appear to the traveler something, he knows not what, of laeta and glabra, of joyous and serene, in our very faces. Else to what end does the world go on, and why was America discovered?

To Americans I hardly need to say—

"Westward the star of empire takes its way."

As a true patriot, I should be ashamed to think that Adam in paradise was more favorably situated on the whole than the backwoodsman in this country.

Our sympathies in Massachusetts are not confined to New England; though we may be estranged from the South, we sympathize with the West. There is the home of the younger sons, as among the Scandinavians they took to the sea for their inheritance. It is too late to be studying Hebrew; it is more important to understand even the slang of today.

Some months ago I went to see a panorama of the Rhine. It was like a dream of the Middle Ages. I floated down its historic stream in something more than imagination, under bridges built by the Romans, and repaired by later heroes, past cities and castles whose very names were music to my ears, and each of which was the subject of a legend. There were Ehrenbreitstein and Rolandseck and Coblentz, which I knew only in history. They were ruins that interested me chiefly. There seemed to come up from its waters and its vine-clad hills and valleys a hushed music as of Crusaders departing for the Holy Land. I floated along under the spell of enchantment, as if I had been transported to an heroic age, and breathed an atmosphere of chivalry.

Soon after, I went to see a panorama of the Mississippi, and as I worked my way up the river in the light of today, and saw the steamboats wooding up, counted the rising cities, gazed on the fresh ruins of Nauvoo, beheld the Indians moving west across the stream, and, as before I had looked up the Moselle, now looked up the Ohio and the Missouri and heard the legends of Dubuque and of Wenona's Cliff—still thinking more of the future than of the past or present—I saw that this was a Rhine stream of a different kind; that the foundations of castles were yet to be laid, and the famous bridges were yet to be thrown over the river; and I felt that THIS WAS THE HEROIC AGE ITSELF, though we know it not, for the hero is commonly the simplest and obscurest of men.

The West of which I speak is but another name for the Wild; and what I have been preparing to say is, that in Wildness is the preservation of the World. Every tree sends its fibers forth in search of the Wild. The cities import it at any price. Men plow and sail for it. From the forest and wilderness come the tonics and barks which brace mankind. Our ancestors were savages. The story of Romulus and Remus being suckled by a wolf is not a meaningless fable. The founders of every state which has risen to eminence have drawn their nourishment and vigor from a similar wild source. It was because the children of the Empire were not suckled by the wolf that they were conquered and displaced by the children of the northern forests who were.

I believe in the forest, and in the meadow, and in the night in which the corn grows. We require an infusion of hemlock, spruce or arbor vitae in our tea. There is a difference between eating and drinking for strength and from mere gluttony. The Hottentots eagerly devour the marrow of the koodoo and other antelopes raw, as a matter of course. Some of our northern Indians eat raw the marrow of the Arctic reindeer, as well as various other parts, including the summits of the antlers, as long as they are soft. And herein, perchance, they have stolen a march on the cooks of Paris. They get what usually goes to feed the fire. This is probably better than stall-fed beef and slaughterhouse pork to make a man of. Give me a wildness whose glance no civilization can endure—as if we lived on the marrow of koodoos devoured raw.

There are some intervals which border the strain of the wood thrush, to which I would migrate—wild lands where no settler has squatted; to which, methinks, I am already acclimated.

The African hunter Cumming tells us that the skin of the eland, as well as that of most other antelopes just killed, emits the most delicious perfume of trees and grass. I would have every man so much like a wild antelope, so much a part and parcel of nature, that his very person should thus sweetly advertise our senses of his presence, and remind us of those parts of nature which he most haunts. I feel no disposition to be satirical, when the trapper's coat emits the odor of musquash even; it is a sweeter scent to me than that which commonly exhales from the merchant's or the scholar's garments. When I go into their wardrobes and handle their vestments, I am reminded of no grassy plains and flowery meads which they have frequented, but of dusty merchants' exchanges and libraries rather.

A tanned skin is something more than respectable, and perhaps olive is a fitter color than white for a man—a denizen of the woods. "The pale white man!" I do not wonder that the African pitied him. Darwin the naturalist says, "A white man bathing by the side of a Tahitian was like a plant bleached by the gardener's art, compared with a fine, dark green one, growing vigorously in the open fields."

Ben Jonson exclaims,—

"How near to good is what is fair!"

So I would say,—

"How near to good is what is WILD!"

Life consists with wildness. The most alive is the wildest. Not yet subdued to man, its presence refreshes him. One who pressed forward incessantly and never rested from his labors, who grew fast and made infinite demands on life, would always find himself in a new country or wilderness, and surrounded by the raw material of life. He would be climbing over the prostrate stems of primitive forest trees.

Hope and the future for me are not in lawns and cultivated fields, not in towns and cities, but in the impervious and quaking swamps. When, formerly, I have analyzed my partiality for some farm which I had contemplated purchasing, I have frequently found that I was attracted solely by a few square rods of impermeable and unfathomable bog—a natural sink in one corner of it. That was the jewel which dazzled me. I derive more of my subsistence from the swamps which surround my native town than from the cultivated gardens in the village. There are no richer parterres to my eyes than the dense beds of dwarf andromeda (Cassandra calyculata) which cover these tender places on the earth's surface. Botany cannot go farther than tell me the names of the shrubs which grow there—the high blueberry, panicled andromeda, lambkill, azalea, and rhodora—all standing in the quaking sphagnum. I often think that I should like to have my house front on this mass of dull red bushes, omitting other flower plots and borders, transplanted spruce and trim box, even graveled walks—to have this fertile spot under my windows, not a few imported barrowfuls of soil only to cover the sand which was thrown out in digging the cellar. Why not put my house, my parlor, behind this plot, instead of behind that meager assemblage of curiosities, that poor apology for a Nature and Art, which I call my front yard? It is an effort to clear up and make a decent appearance when the carpenter and mason have departed, though done as much for the passer-by as the dweller within. The most tasteful front-yard fence was never an agreeable object of study to me; the most elaborate ornaments, acorn tops, or what not, soon wearied and disgusted me. Bring your sills up to the very edge of the swamp, then (though it may not be the best place for a dry cellar), so that there be no access on that side to citizens. Front yards are not made to walk in, but, at most, through, and you could go in the back way.

Yes, though you may think me perverse, if it were proposed to me to dwell in the neighborhood of the most beautiful garden that ever human art contrived, or else of a Dismal Swamp, I should certainly decide for the swamp. How vain, then, have been all your labors, citizens, for me!

My spirits infallibly rise in proportion to the outward dreariness. Give me the ocean, the desert, or the wilderness! In the desert, pure air and solitude compensate for want of moisture and fertility. The traveler Burton says of it—"Your MORALE improves; you become frank and cordial, hospitable and single-minded.... In the desert, spirituous liquors excite only disgust. There is a keen enjoyment in a mere animal existence." They who have been traveling long on the steppes of Tartary say, "On re-entering cultivated lands, the agitation, perplexity, and turmoil of civilization oppressed and suffocated us; the air seemed to fail us, and we felt every moment as if about to die of asphyxia." When I would recreate myself, I seek the darkest woods the thickest and most interminable and, to the citizen, most dismal, swamp. I enter a swamp as a sacred place,— a sanctum sanctorum. There is the strength, the marrow, of Nature. The wildwood covers the virgin mould,—and the same soil is good for men and for trees. A man's health requires as many acres of meadow to his prospect as his farm does loads of muck. There are the strong meats on which he feeds. A town is saved, not more by the righteous men in it than by the woods and swamps that surround it. A township where one primitive forest waves above while another primitive forest rots below—such a town is fitted to raise not only corn and potatoes, but poets and philosophers for the coming ages. In such a soil grew Homer and Confucius and the rest, and out of such a wilderness comes the Reformer eating locusts and wild honey.

To preserve wild animals implies generally the creation of a forest for them to dwell in or resort to. So it is with man. A hundred years ago they sold bark in our streets peeled from our own woods. In the very aspect of those primitive and rugged trees there was, methinks, a tanning principle which hardened and consolidated the fibers of men's thoughts. Ah! already I shudder for these comparatively degenerate days of my native village, when you cannot collect a load of bark of good thickness, and we no longer produce tar and turpentine.

The civilized nations—Greece, Rome, England—have been sustained by the primitive forests which anciently rotted where they stand. They survive as long as the soil is not exhausted. Alas for human culture! little is to be expected of a nation, when the vegetable mould is exhausted, and it is compelled to make manure of the bones of its fathers. There the poet sustains himself merely by his own superfluous fat, and the philosopher comes down on his marrow-bones.

It is said to be the task of the American "to work the virgin soil," and that "agriculture here already assumes proportions unknown everywhere else." I think that the farmer displaces the Indian even because he redeems the meadow, and so makes himself stronger and in some respects more natural. I was surveying for a man the other day a single straight line one hundred and thirty-two rods long, through a swamp at whose entrance might have been written the words which Dante read over the entrance to the infernal regions,—"Leave all hope, ye that enter"—that is, of ever getting out again; where at one time I saw my employer actually up to his neck and swimming for his life in his property, though it was still winter. He had another similar swamp which I could not survey at all, because it was completely under water, and nevertheless, with regard to a third swamp, which I did SURVEY from a distance, he remarked to me, true to his instincts, that he would not part with it for any consideration, on account of the mud which it contained. And that man intends to put a girdling ditch round the whole in the course of forty months, and so redeem it by the magic of his spade. I refer to him only as the type of a class.

The weapons with which we have gained our most important victories, which should be handed down as heirlooms from father to son, are not the sword and the lance, but the bushwhack, the turf-cutter, the spade, and the bog hoe, rusted with the blood of many a meadow, and begrimed with the dust of many a hard-fought field. The very winds blew the Indian's cornfield into the meadow, and pointed out the way which he had not the skill to follow. He had no better implement with which to intrench himself in the land than a clam-shell. But the farmer is armed with plow and spade.

In literature it is only the wild that attracts us. Dullness is but another name for tameness. It is the uncivilized free and wild thinking in Hamlet and the Iliad, in all the scriptures and mythologies, not learned in the schools, that delights us. As the wild duck is more swift and beautiful than the tame, so is the wild—the mallard—thought, which 'mid falling dews wings its way above the fens. A truly good book is something as natural, and as unexpectedly and unaccountably fair and perfect, as a wild-flower discovered on the prairies of the West or in the jungles of the East. Genius is a light which makes the darkness visible, like the lightning's flash, which perchance shatters the temple of knowledge itself—and not a taper lighted at the hearthstone of the race, which pales before the light of common day.

English literature, from the days of the minstrels to the Lake Poets—Chaucer and Spenser and Milton, and even Shakespeare, included—breathes no quite fresh and, in this sense, wild strain. It is an essentially tame and civilized literature, reflecting Greece and Rome. Her wilderness is a green wood, her wild man a Robin Hood. There is plenty of genial love of Nature, but not so much of Nature herself. Her chronicles inform us when her wild animals, but not when the wild man in her, became extinct.

The science of Humboldt is one thing, poetry is another thing. The poet today, notwithstanding all the discoveries of science, and the accumulated learning of mankind, enjoys no advantage over Homer.

Where is the literature which gives expression to Nature? He would be a poet who could impress the winds and streams into his service, to speak for him; who nailed words to their primitive senses, as farmers drive down stakes in the spring, which the frost has heaved; who derived his words as often as he used them—transplanted them to his page with earth adhering to their roots; whose words were so true and fresh and natural that they would appear to expand like the buds at the approach of spring, though they lay half smothered between two musty leaves in a library—aye, to bloom and bear fruit there, after their kind, annually, for the faithful reader, in sympathy with surrounding Nature.

I do not know of any poetry to quote which adequately expresses this yearning for the Wild. Approached from this side, the best poetry is tame. I do not know where to find in any literature, ancient or modern, any account which contents me of that Nature with which even I am acquainted. You will perceive that I demand something which no Augustan nor Elizabethan age, which no culture, in short, can give. Mythology comes nearer to it than anything. How much more fertile a Nature, at least, has Grecian mythology its root in than English literature! Mythology is the crop which the Old World bore before its soil was exhausted, before the fancy and imagination were affected with blight; and which it still bears, wherever its pristine vigor is unabated. All other literatures endure only as the elms which overshadow our houses; but this is like the great dragon-tree of the Western Isles, as old as mankind, and, whether that does or not, will endure as long; for the decay of other literatures makes the soil in which it thrives.

The West is preparing to add its fables to those of the East. The valleys of the Ganges, the Nile, and the Shine having yielded their crop, it remains to be seen what the valleys of the Amazon, the Plate, the Orinoco, the St. Lawrence, and the Mississippi will produce. Perchance, when, in the course of ages, American liberty has become a fiction of the past—as it is to some extent a fiction of the present—the poets of the world will be inspired by American mythology.

The wildest dreams of wild men, even, are not the less true, though they may not recommend themselves to the sense which is most common among Englishmen and Americans today. It is not every truth that recommends itself to the common sense. Nature has a place for the wild Clematis as well as for the cabbage. Some expressions of truth are reminiscent—others merely SENSIBLE, as the phrase is,—others prophetic. Some forms of disease, even, may prophesy forms of health. The geologist has discovered that the figures of serpents, griffins, flying dragons, and other fanciful embellishments of heraldry, have their prototypes in the forms of fossil species which were extinct before man was created, and hence "indicate a faint and shadowy knowledge of a previous state of organic existence." The Hindus dreamed that the earth rested on an elephant, and the elephant on a tortoise, and the tortoise on a serpent; and though it may be an unimportant coincidence, it will not be out of place here to state, that a fossil tortoise has lately been discovered in Asia large enough to support an elephant. I confess that I am partial to these wild fancies, which transcend the order of time and development. They are the sublimest recreation of the intellect. The partridge loves peas, but not those that go with her into the pot.

In short, all good things are wild and free. There is something in a strain of music, whether produced by an instrument or by the human voice—take the sound of a bugle in a summer night, for instance—which by its wildness, to speak without satire, reminds me of the cries emitted by wild beasts in their native forests. It is so much of their wildness as I can understand. Give me for my friends and neighbors wild men, not tame ones. The wildness of the savage is but a faint symbol of the awful ferity with which good men and lovers meet.

I love even to see the domestic animals reassert their native rights—any evidence that they have not wholly lost their original wild habits and vigor; as when my neighbor's cow breaks out of her pasture early in the spring and boldly swims the river, a cold, gray tide, twenty-five or thirty rods wide, swollen by the melted snow. It is the buffalo crossing the Mississippi. This exploit confers some dignity on the herd in my eyes—already dignified. The seeds of instinct are preserved under the thick hides of cattle and horses, like seeds in the bowels of the earth, an indefinite period.

Any sportiveness in cattle is unexpected. I saw one day a herd of a dozen bullocks and cows running about and frisking in unwieldy sport, like huge rats, even like kittens. They shook their heads, raised their tails, and rushed up and down a hill, and I perceived by their horns, as well as by their activity, their relation to the deer tribe. But, alas! a sudden loud WHOA! would have damped their ardor at once, reduced them from venison to beef, and stiffened their sides and sinews like the locomotive. Who but the Evil One has cried "Whoa!" to mankind? Indeed, the life of cattle, like that of many men, is but a sort of locomotiveness; they move a side at a time, and man, by his machinery, is meeting the horse and the ox halfway. Whatever part the whip has touched is thenceforth palsied. Who would ever think of a SIDE of any of the supple cat tribe, as we speak of a SIDE of beef?

I rejoice that horses and steers have to be broken before they can be made the slaves of men, and that men themselves have some wild oats still left to sow before they become submissive members of society. Undoubtedly, all men are not equally fit subjects for civilization; and because the majority, like dogs and sheep, are tame by inherited disposition, this is no reason why the others should have their natures broken that they may be reduced to the same level. Men are in the main alike, but they were made several in order that they might be various. If a low use is to be served, one man will do nearly or quite as well as another; if a high one, individual excellence is to be regarded. Any man can stop a hole to keep the wind away, but no other man could serve so rare a use as the author of this illustration did. Confucius says,—"The skins of the tiger and the leopard, when they are tanned, are as the skins of the dog and the sheep tanned." But it is not the part of a true culture to tame tigers, any more than it is to make sheep ferocious; and tanning their skins for shoes is not the best use to which they can be put.

When looking over a list of men's names in a foreign language, as of military officers, or of authors who have written on a particular subject, I am reminded once more that there is nothing in a name. The name Menschikoff, for instance, has nothing in it to my ears more human than a whisker, and it may belong to a rat. As the names of the Poles and Russians are to us, so are ours to them. It is as if they had been named by the child's rigmarole,—IERY FIERY ICHERY VAN, TITTLE-TOL-TAN. I see in my mind a herd of wild creatures swarming over the earth, and to each the herdsman has affixed some barbarous sound in his own dialect. The names of men are, of course, as cheap and meaningless as BOSE and TRAY, the names of dogs.

Methinks it would be some advantage to philosophy if men were named merely in the gross, as they are known. It would be necessary only to know the genus and perhaps the race or variety, to know the individual. We are not prepared to believe that every private soldier in a Roman army had a name of his own—because we have not supposed that he had a character of his own.

At present our only true names are nicknames. I knew a boy who, from his peculiar energy, was called "Buster" by his playmates, and this rightly supplanted his Christian name. Some travelers tell us that an Indian had no name given him at first, but earned it, and his name was his fame; and among some tribes he acquired a new name with every new exploit. It is pitiful when a man bears a name for convenience merely, who has earned neither name nor fame.

I will not allow mere names to make distinctions for me, but still see men in herds for all them. A familiar name cannot make a man less strange to me. It may be given to a savage who retains in secret his own wild title earned in the woods. We have a wild savage in us, and a savage name is perchance somewhere recorded as ours. I see that my neighbor, who bears the familiar epithet William or Edwin, takes it off with his jacket. It does not adhere to him when asleep or in anger, or aroused by any passion or inspiration. I seem to hear pronounced by some of his kin at such a time his original wild name in some jaw-breaking or else melodious tongue.

Here is this vast, savage, hovering mother of ours, Nature, lying all around, with such beauty, and such affection for her children, as the leopard; and yet we are so early weaned from her breast to society, to that culture which is exclusively an interaction of man on man—a sort of breeding in and in, which produces at most a merely English nobility, a civilization destined to have a speedy limit.

In society, in the best institutions of men, it is easy to detect a certain precocity. When we should still be growing children, we are already little men. Give me a culture which imports much muck from the meadows, and deepens the soil—not that which trusts to heating manures, and improved implements and modes of culture only!

Many a poor sore-eyed student that I have heard of would grow faster, both intellectually and physically, if, instead of sitting up so very late, he honestly slumbered a fool's allowance.

There may be an excess even of informing light. Niepce, a Frenchman, discovered "actinism," that power in the sun's rays which produces a chemical effect; that granite rocks, and stone structures, and statues of metal "are all alike destructively acted upon during the hours of sunshine, and, but for provisions of Nature no less wonderful, would soon perish under the delicate touch of the most subtle of the agencies of the universe." But he observed that "those bodies which underwent this change during the daylight possessed the power of restoring themselves to their original conditions during the hours of night, when this excitement was no longer influencing them." Hence it has been inferred that "the hours of darkness are as necessary to the inorganic creation as we know night and sleep are to the organic kingdom." Not even does the moon shine every night, but gives place to darkness.

I would not have every man nor every part of a man cultivated, any more than I would have every acre of earth cultivated: part will be tillage, but the greater part will be meadow and forest, not only serving an immediate use, but preparing a mould against a distant future, by the annual decay of the vegetation which it supports.

There are other letters for the child to learn than those which Cadmus invented. The Spaniards have a good term to express this wild and dusky knowledge—Gramatica parda—tawny grammar, a kind of mother-wit derived from that same leopard to which I have referred.

We have heard of a Society for the Diffusion of Useful Knowledge. It is said that knowledge is power, and the like. Methinks there is equal need of a Society for the Diffusion of Useful Ignorance, what we will call Beautiful Knowledge, a knowledge useful in a higher sense: for what is most of our boasted so-called knowledge but a conceit that we know something, which robs us of the advantage of our actual ignorance? What we call knowledge is often our positive ignorance; ignorance our negative knowledge. By long years of patient industry and reading of the newspapers—for what are the libraries of science but files of newspapers—a man accumulates a myriad facts, lays them up in his memory, and then when in some spring of his life he saunters abroad into the Great Fields of thought, he, as it were, goes to grass like a horse and leaves all his harness behind in the stable. I would say to the Society for the Diffusion of Useful Knowledge, sometimes,—Go to grass. You have eaten hay long enough. The spring has come with its green crop. The very cows are driven to their country pastures before the end of May; though I have heard of one unnatural farmer who kept his cow in the barn and fed her on hay all the year round. So, frequently, the Society for the Diffusion of Useful Knowledge treats its cattle.

A man's ignorance sometimes is not only useful, but beautiful—while his knowledge, so called, is oftentimes worse than useless, besides being ugly. Which is the best man to deal with—he who knows nothing about a subject, and, what is extremely rare, knows that he knows nothing, or he who really knows something about it, but thinks that he knows all?

My desire for knowledge is intermittent, but my desire to bathe my head in atmospheres unknown to my feet is perennial and constant. The highest that we can attain to is not Knowledge, but Sympathy with Intelligence. I do not know that this higher knowledge amounts to anything more definite than a novel and grand surprise on a sudden revelation of the insufficiency of all that we called Knowledge before—a discovery that there are more things in heaven and earth than are dreamed of in our philosophy. It is the lighting up of the mist by the sun. Man cannot KNOW in any higher sense than this, any more than he can look serenely and with impunity in the face of the sun: "You will not perceive that, as perceiving a particular thing," say the Chaldean Oracles.

There is something servile in the habit of seeking after a law which we may obey. We may study the laws of matter at and for our onvenience, but a successful life knows no law. It is an unfortunate discovery certainly, that of a law which binds us where we did not know before that we were bound. Live free, child of the mist—and with respect to knowledge we are all children of the mist. The man who takes the liberty to live is superior to all the laws, by virtue of his relation to the lawmaker. "That is active duty," says the Vishnu Purana, "which is not for our bondage; that is knowledge which is for our liberation: all other duty is good only unto weariness; all other knowledge is only the cleverness of an artist."

It is remarkable how few events or crises there are in our histories, how little exercised we have been in our minds, how few experiences we have had. I would fain be assured that I am growing apace and rankly, though my very growth disturb this dull equanimity—though it be with struggle through long, dark, muggy nights or seasons of gloom. It would be well if all our lives were a divine tragedy even, instead of this trivial comedy or farce. Dante, Bunyan, and others appear to have been exercised in their minds more than we: they were subjected to a kind of culture such as our district schools and colleges do not contemplate. Even Mahomet, though many may scream at his name, had a good deal more to live for, aye, and to die for, than they have commonly.

When, at rare intervals, some thought visits one, as perchance he is walking on a railroad, then, indeed, the cars go by without his hearing them. But soon, by some inexorable law, our life goes by and the cars return.

"Gentle breeze, that wanderest unseen,
And bendest the thistles round Loira of storms,
Traveler of the windy glens,
Why hast thou left my ear so soon?"

While almost all men feel an attraction drawing them to society, few are attracted strongly to Nature. In their reaction to Nature men appear to me for the most part, notwithstanding their arts, lower than the animals. It is not often a beautiful relation, as in the case of the animals. How little appreciation of the beauty of the land-scape there is among us! We have to be told that the Greeks called the world Beauty, or Order, but we do not see clearly why they did so, and we esteem it at best only a curious philological fact.

For my part, I feel that with regard to Nature I live a sort of border life, on the confines of a world into which I make occasional and transient forays only, and my patriotism and allegiance to the state into whose territories I seem to retreat are those of a moss-trooper. Unto a life which I call natural I would gladly follow even a will-o'-the-wisp through bogs and sloughs unimaginable, but no moon nor firefly has shown me the causeway to it. Nature is a personality so vast and universal that we have never seen one of her features. The walker in the familiar fields which stretch around my native town sometimes finds himself in another land than is described in their owners' deeds, as it were in some faraway field on the confines of the actual Concord, where her jurisdiction ceases, and the idea which the word Concord suggests ceases to be suggested. These farms which I have myself surveyed, these bounds which I have set up, appear dimly still as through a mist; but they have no chemistry to fix them; they fade from the surface of the glass, and the picture which the painter painted stands out dimly from beneath. The world with which we are commonly acquainted leaves no trace, and it will have no anniversary.

I took a walk on Spaulding's Farm the other afternoon. I saw the setting sun lighting up the opposite side of a stately pine wood. Its golden rays straggled into the aisles of the wood as into some noble hall. I was impressed as if some ancient and altogether admirable and shining family had settled there in that part of the land called Concord, unknown to me—to whom the sun was servant—who had not gone into society in the village—who had not been called on. I saw their park, their pleasure-ground, beyond through the wood, in Spaulding's cranberry-meadow. The pines furnished them with gables as they grew. Their house was not obvious to vision; the trees grew through it. I do not know whether I heard the sounds of a suppressed hilarity or not. They seemed to recline on the sunbeams. They have sons and daughters. They are quite well. The farmer's cart-path, which leads directly through their hall, does not in the least put them out, as the muddy bottom of a pool is sometimes seen through the reflected skies. They never heard of Spaulding, and do not know that he is their neighbor—notwithstanding I heard him whistle as he drove his team through the house. Nothing can equal the serenity of their lives. Their coat-of-arms is simply a lichen. I saw it painted on the pines and oaks. Their attics were in the tops of the trees. They are of no politics. There was no noise of labor. I did not perceive that they were weaving or spinning. Yet I did detect, when the wind lulled and hearing was done away, the finest imaginable sweet musical hum,—as of a distant hive in May, which perchance was the sound of their thinking. They had no idle thoughts, and no one without could see their work, for their industry was not as in knots and excrescences embayed.

But I find it difficult to remember them. They fade irrevocably out of my mind even now while I speak, and endeavor to recall them and recollect myself. It is only after a long and serious effort to recollect my best thoughts that I become again aware of their cohabitancy. If it were not for such families as this, I think I should move out of Concord.

We are accustomed to say in New England that few and fewer pigeons visit us every year. Our forests furnish no mast for them. So, it would seem, few and fewer thoughts visit each growing man from year to year, for the grove in our minds is laid waste—sold to feed unnecessary fires of ambition, or sent to mill—and there is scarcely a twig left for them to perch on. They no longer build nor breed with us. In some more genial season, perchance, a faint shadow flits across the landscape of the mind, cast by the WINGS of some thought in its vernal or autumnal migration, but, looking up, we are unable to detect the substance of the thought itself. Our winged thoughts are turned to poultry. They no longer soar, and they attain only to a Shanghai and Cochin- China grandeur. Those GRA-A-ATE THOUGHTS, those GRA-A-ATE men you hear of!

We hug the earth—how rarely we mount! Methinks we might elevate ourselves a little more. We might climb a tree, at least. I found my account in climbing a tree once. It was a tall white pine, on the top of a hill; and though I got well pitched, I was well paid for it, for I discovered new mountains in the horizon which I had never seen before—so much more of the earth and the heavens. I might have walked about the foot of the tree for threescore years and ten, and yet I certainly should never have seen them. But, above all, I discovered around me—it was near the end of June—on the ends of the topmost branches only, a few minute and delicate red conelike blossoms, the fertile flower of the white pine looking heavenward. I carried straightway to the village the topmost spire, and showed it to stranger jurymen who walked the streets—for it was court week—and to farmers and lumber-dealers and woodchoppers and hunters, and not one had ever seen the like before, but they wondered as at a star dropped down. Tell of ancient architects finishing their works on the tops of columns as perfectly as on the lower and more visible parts! Nature has from the first expanded the minute blossoms of the forest only toward the heavens, above men's heads and unobserved by them. We see only the flowers that are under our feet in the meadows. The pines have developed their delicate blossoms on the highest twigs of the wood every summer for ages, as well over the heads of Nature's red children as of her white ones; yet scarcely a farmer or hunter in the land has ever seen them.

Above all, we cannot afford not to live in the present. He is blessed over all mortals who loses no moment of the passing life in remembering the past. Unless our philosophy hears the cock crow in every barnyard within our horizon, it is belated. That sound commonly reminds us that we are growing rusty and antique in our employments and habits of thoughts. His philosophy comes down to a more recent time than ours. There is something suggested by it that is a newer testament,—the gospel according to this moment. He has not fallen astern; he has got up early and kept up early, and to be where he is is to be in season, in the foremost rank of time. It is an expression of the health and soundness of Nature, a brag for all the world,—healthiness as of a spring burst forth, a new fountain of the Muses, to celebrate this last instant of time. Where he lives no fugitive slave laws are passed. Who has not betrayed his master many times since last he heard that note?

The merit of this bird's strain is in its freedom from all plaintiveness. The singer can easily move us to tears or to laughter, but where is he who can excite in us a pure morning joy? When, in doleful dumps, breaking the awful stillness of our wooden sidewalk on a Sunday, or, perchance, a watcher in the house of mourning, I hear a cockerel crow far or near, I think to myself, "There is one of us well, at any rate,"—and with a sudden gush return to my senses.

We had a remarkable sunset one day last November. I was walking in a meadow, the source of a small brook, when the sun at last, just before setting, after a cold, gray day, reached a clear stratum in the horizon, and the softest, brightest morning sunlight fell on the dry grass and on the stems of the trees in the opposite horizon and on the leaves of the shrub oaks on the hillside, while our shadows stretched long over the meadow eastward, as if we were the only motes in its beams. It was such a light as we could not have imagined a moment before, and the air also was so warm and serene that nothing was wanting to make a paradise of that meadow. When we reflected that this was not a solitary phenomenon, never to happen again, but that it would happen forever and ever, an infinite number of evenings, and cheer and reassure the latest child that walked there, it was more glorious still.

The sun sets on some retired meadow, where no house is visible, with all the glory and splendor that it lavishes on cities, and perchance as it has never set before—where there is but a solitary marsh hawk to have his wings gilded by it, or only a musquash looks out from his cabin, and there is some little black-veined brook in the midst of the marsh, just beginning to meander, winding slowly round a decaying stump. We walked in so pure and bright a light, gilding the withered grass and leaves, so softly and serenely bright, I thought I had never bathed in such a golden flood, without a ripple or a murmur to it. The west side of every wood and rising ground gleamed like the boundary of Elysium, and the sun on our backs seemed like a gentle herdsman driving us home at evening.

So we saunter toward the Holy Land, till one day the sun shall shine more brightly than ever he has done, shall perchance shine into our minds and hearts, and light up our whole lives with a great awakening light, as warm and serene and golden as on a bankside in autumn.